THIS IS A BORZOI BOOK PUBLISHED BY ALFRED A. KNOPF

Text copyright © 2003 by Natasha Anastasia Tarpley

Illustrations copyright © 2003 by E. B. Lewis

All rights reserved under International and Pan-American Copyright Conventions. Published in the United States of America by Alfred A. Knopf, an imprint of Random House Children's Books, a division of Random House, Inc., New York, and simultaneously in Canada by Random House of Canada Limited, Toronto. Distributed by Random House, Inc., New York.

www.randomhouse.com/kids

KNOPF, BORZOI BOOKS, and the colophon are registered trademarks of Random House, Inc.

Library of Congress Cataloging-in-Publication Data available upon request.

ISBN 0-375-81053-6 (trade) — ISBN 0-375-91053-0 (lib. bdg.)

Manufactured in China

June 2003

10 9 8 7 6 5 4 3 2 1

First Edition

Joe-Joe's First Flight

By Natasha Anastasia Tarpley • Illustrated by E. B. Lewis

Alfred A. Knopf New York

This book is dedicated with love to my Ancestors,
whose perseverance and courage have enabled me to fly.

And to my cousin Rian James Hudson (September 16, 1981–July 29, 1998).
I hope you've found your wings. We miss you.

Special thanks also to pilots
Jim Barr, Ed Jones, and Perry Smith,
for teaching me all about airplanes and the mechanics of flight.

—N.A.T.

To Bryon Stewart and the pilots of the flying circus.
Thanks for giving this book its wings.

—E.B.L.

They say the people could fly. . . .

—*Virginia Hamilton*

I live in a town called Blind Eye

with Daddy, Mama, and baby sister, June.

We have a house on a piece of land that goes on and on until it meets the sky. My daddy worked hard on that land for most of his life, planting, plowing, and harvesting crops, just to make ends meet for our family.

Where our land ends and the sky begins, there is an airport. It's got a big barn where the planes are kept, a shed for an office, and a wide field where the planes take off and land.

On the day that I was born, August 26, 1922, the first plane to ever fly out of Blind Eye's airport took flight. Everyone in Blind Eye gathered on our land that day. They were all so excited and proud of our little airport.

Every time after that, whenever the planes would fly overhead, Daddy would carry me outside and hold me up so that I could see the planes taking off. 'Course, I don't remember too good, I was just a baby then. But Daddy tells me that planes flying through the sky were some of the first things I saw in the world, aside from his and Mama's faces.

Daddy's wanted to fly ever since, and so have I.

"Working the air sure beats working the earth any day," Daddy says.

Soon after that first flight, Daddy and some of his friends got jobs at the airport. There was Henry, Pete, Charlie, and Paul-Michael. They named themselves the All-Original Flying Men, though they've never had the chance to fly a plane.

But Daddy and me, we talk about flying all the time.
We dream together.

In the morning, before Daddy leaves for work, he spins
me around, fast, faster, faster. My arms open to the wind,
I imagine that I'm taking off, just like a plane. Then
Daddy sets me gently on the ground. "A smooth landing,"
he says, and kisses me goodbye.

When Daddy comes home at the end of the day, we sit and watch the planes land at the airport, the last of the sun sparkling on their wings. We wonder how far they've traveled, all the places they must have been.

"The Flying Men were the first black men ever to work at the airport, maybe even set foot on a plane. The whole town was proud of us." Daddy's face lights up. "Everyone was so excited that we would have the chance to fly!"

"When will you get to fly, Daddy?" I ask. Suddenly, the twinkle fades from Daddy's eye.

"Well, son, I ask the man, and I keep on asking. But all he says is 'in due time.' Seems like the time is *never* due," Daddy says sadly.

"That's not fair, Daddy!" I'm so mad I can feel tears welling up in my eyes.

"No, it's not fair, Joe-Joe. And it's not right." Daddy gently lifts my chin.

"But you just wait. Our chance is coming."

By the time Daddy finishes his story, the sky is pitch-black.

See, in Blind Eye, at night, the darkness is so thick you can't see your hand in front of your face.

Daddy tells me that every year the Flying Men can't fly, the folks in Blind Eye lose a little bit of hope. All that lost hope formed a cloud over the town, and now even the moonlight and the stars can't break through.

"Daddy, show me your wings," I whisper.
Daddy reaches deep into his back pocket
and pulls out a folded white handkerchief.
Inside is the tiny pair of gold wings that
Daddy got when he first started working at
the airport.
 He gives them a
good wipe with the
handkerchief, then
places them carefully in my
palm. They're so pretty and
shiny. It's like holding a
miniature star. "Give 'em a
wish," Daddy says. I close my eyes
and wish the same thing I always do: to fly.
And to bring the moon back to Blind Eye.

Sometimes I help the Flying Men with their work. They repair the body, the wings, and the engines of the planes. They clean the insides and the windows, and load the cargo. They know everything there is to know about airplanes.

One evening, as the Flying Men are tying down the planes for the night, all anybody can talk about is flying, like an itch you can't scratch.

"Wouldn't it be nice to be up there, soaring through the moonlight." Daddy sighs, staring off into the darkness.

"But the moon don't come around here no more." Henry shrugs his shoulders.

"We should get Joe-Joe to call her. He could get the moon to come for sure." Paul-Michael winks at me.

"Now, don't go giving him any crazy ideas." Daddy frowns.

But I start thinking, real quiet to myself. I could get the
moon to come, sing her a song or something. I make up
my mind right then and there. I slip away and head
toward the little plane parked near the runway.

I climb into the cockpit and stretch back on the seat
to make my plan. Soon my eyelids start to feel heavy
and I let my eyes close. As I drift off to sleep,
I can see myself turn on the ignition switch
on the control panel and set the throttle.

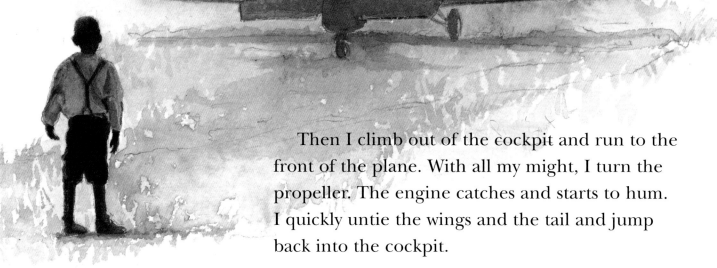

Then I climb out of the cockpit and run to the
front of the plane. With all my might, I turn the
propeller. The engine catches and starts to hum.
I quickly untie the wings and the tail and jump
back into the cockpit.

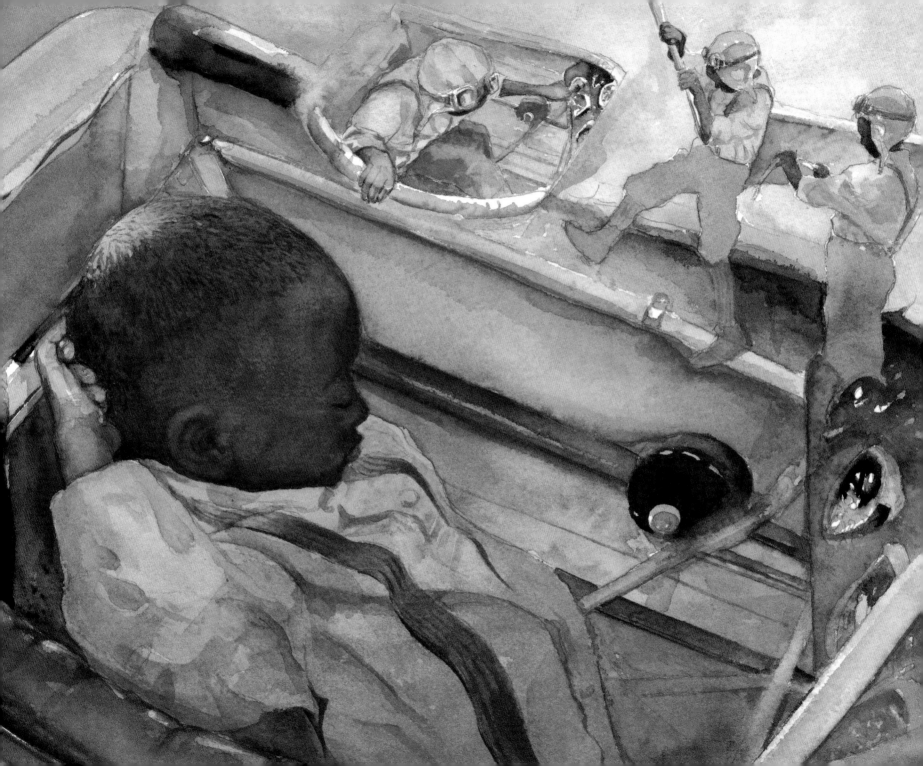

I pull the chocks away from the airplane wheels and
I'm off! Moving slowly at first, but picking up speed. The
engine roars and the propeller spins so fast it's a blur.
    I'm too far to catch by the time Daddy notices I'm
gone and starts calling my name.

Fast . . .
faster . . .
faster . . .
whooooosh!

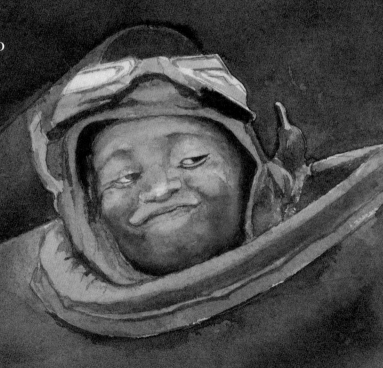

I pull back on the control stick and the plane begins to lift. Before I know it, the ground drops from beneath me. My heart jumps into my throat and my stomach sinks to my feet.

I can't see anything ahead of me it's so dark, but I keep climbing. The plane wobbles some, but I steady her. Higher and higher I go. "I'm flying!" I shout, but the wind gobbles up my words as soon as they leave my mouth.

Never mind, I'm floating free, riding the air. Nothing but the sky and me!

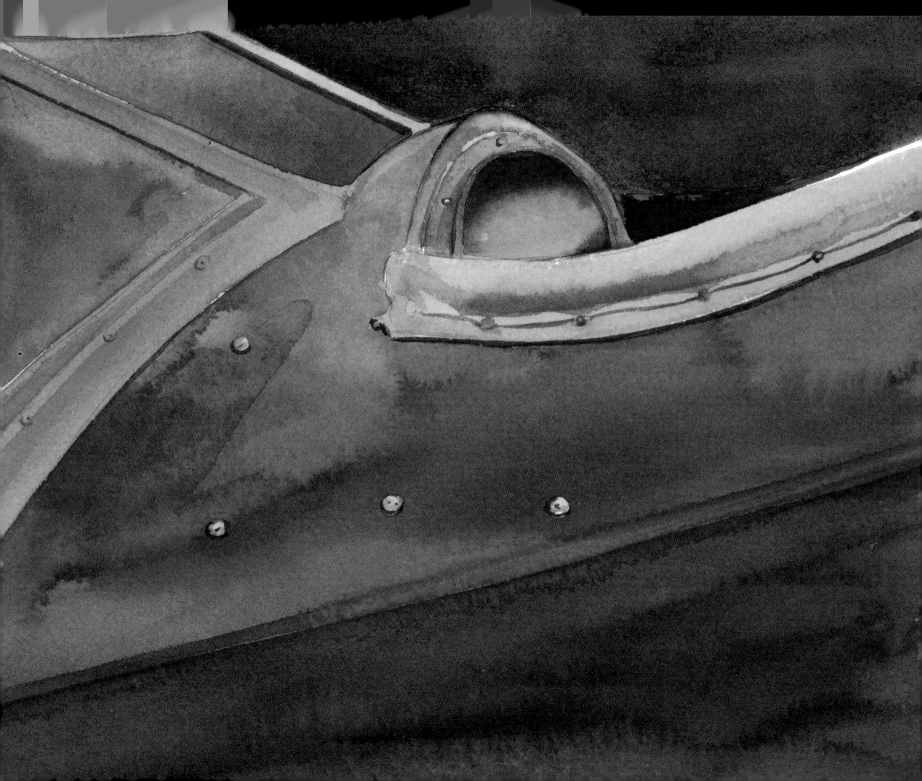

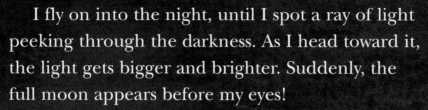

I fly on into the night, until I spot a ray of light
peeking through the darkness. As I head toward it,
the light gets bigger and brighter. Suddenly, the
full moon appears before my eyes!

   I fly as close as I can and start singing the song
I made up just for her.

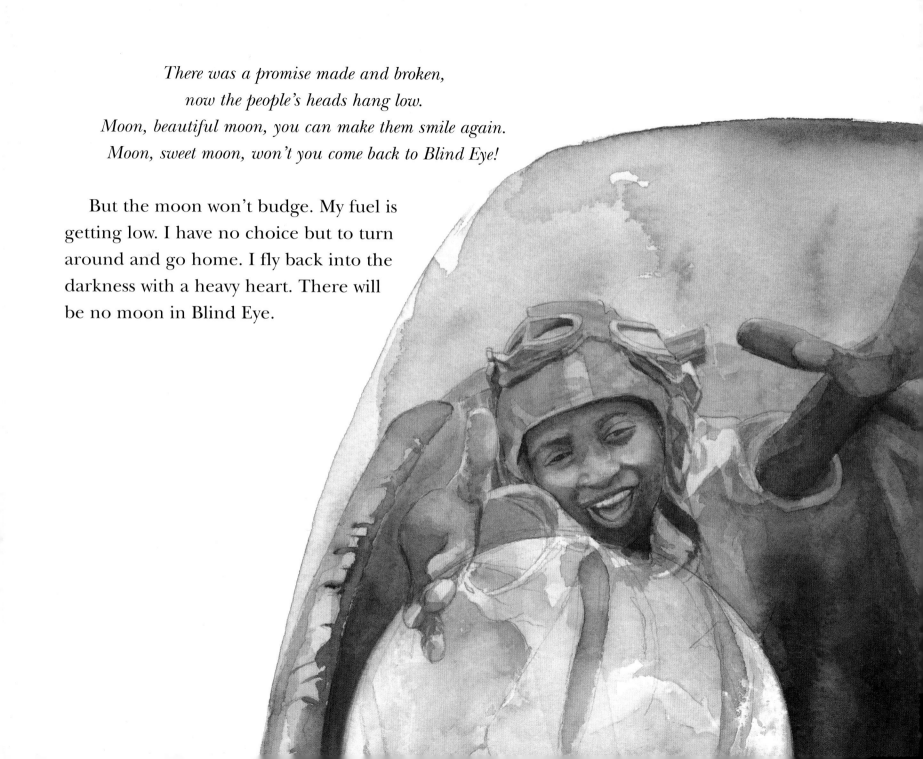

There was a promise made and broken,
now the people's heads hang low.
Moon, beautiful moon, you can make them smile again.
Moon, sweet moon, won't you come back to Blind Eye!

But the moon won't budge. My fuel is
getting low. I have no choice but to turn
around and go home. I fly back into the
darkness with a heavy heart. There will
be no moon in Blind Eye.

Then, out of the corner of my eye, I see a flash of light. I turn to look behind me and shout for joy when I see it's the moon following me! I slow down to let her catch up, and we ride into Blind Eye together.

The moon lights up the sky, bright as daytime. I can see our little house and our land; there's the store, the church, and my school. But I don't stop. I fly on toward the airport.

Down below, all of Blind Eye has
gathered on the field. There's Daddy,
Mama, Baby June, and the Flying Men, too.

The Flying Men light torches along the
runway so I can see where to land. I line
up the plane with the runway; then I start
my descent. I'm going so slow now, it feels
like the plane is just hanging in the air.
I turn back and wave at the moon one
more time as I near the ground.

The flames of the torches, which
looked like matchsticks from the sky, are
now as large and bright as burning
bushes; and the people, who looked small
enough to hold in my hand, have grown
into their tall selves again.

Blades of grass fan out and flatten beneath the plane's
wind. The wheels touch down with a thump and a jolt,
and I'm back on the ground.

The plane rolls to a stop. Everybody rushes toward me,
cheering and calling my name. Folks are singing and
celebrating just like they did the day of the very first flight.

Daddy lifts me out of the plane and into his arms. "Why'd you have to go and do such a foolish thing, Joe-Joe?" He grins up at me.

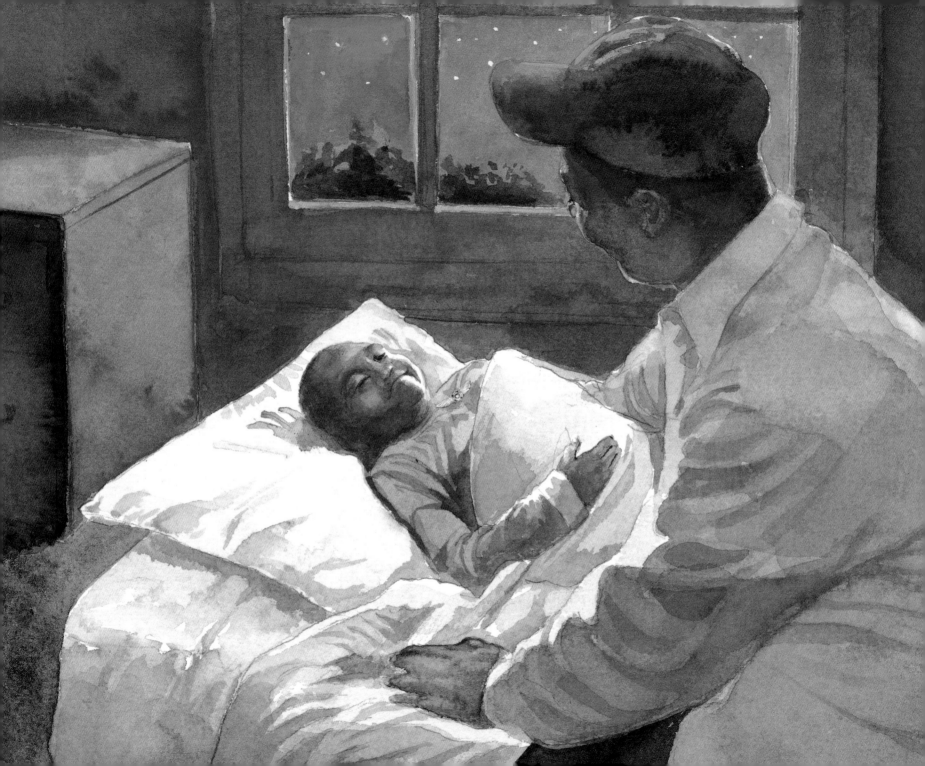

Daddy carries me like that all the way home.

Later, when he tucks me in, Daddy pins his tiny gold wings onto my pajamas. "You're a Flying Man now, son," he says.

I look out my window at the moon, full and round in the sky.
She winks at me, a promise that she'll never leave us.

Author's Note

As a little girl, I had the flying bug—bad! I'd make a cape out of my mother's clean towels and jump down the stairs or out of the small apple tree that grew in our backyard, flapping my arms as fast as I could. Other times, I'd twirl around and around until I was so dizzy I really did feel as if I were floating. Of course, all that these stunts ever got me was sore ankles and headaches. But when I got older and started reading books about flying, I learned that my desire to fly wasn't so strange after all.

Ever since there have been human beings on the earth and a sky above our heads, people have wanted to fly. But I also learned that in the early days of aviation, African Americans were denied the opportunity to make their dreams of flying a reality.

Orville and Wilbur Wright's historic powered-airplane flight in 1903 marked the beginning of the modern aviation industry and sparked widespread enthusiasm about the possibilities of flight. However, as were most other areas of life during the early twentieth century, the field of aviation was segregated. Blacks were not accepted at American flight schools, nor were they eligible to receive United States military flight training. Even well into the 1960s and beyond, African American pilots faced racial discrimination when seeking employment with commercial airlines.

Still, those African Americans who were determined to fly soared beyond these obstacles to achieve their goals. In 1917, Eugene Bullard, who left America to join the French Foreign Legion, flew with the French during World War I. In 1921, a young woman named Bessie Coleman became the first licensed black pilot in the United States, after being trained at flight schools in France because the U.S. schools would not accept her. Bullard's and Coleman's success inspired generations of black men and women to pursue careers in aviation.

In the 1930s, black flying clubs were organized in Los Angeles and Chicago. John C. Robinson, who founded the Chicago club, built its first airstrip in the black township of Robbins, Illinois. Robinson later went on to advise Emperor Haile Selassie on building an Ethiopian air force. Cornelius R. Coffey started the Coffey School of Aeronautics in Illinois, which offered flight instruction to African American students. And pilots C. Alfred Anderson and Dr. Albert E. Forsythe became the first African Americans to complete a round-trip transcontinental flight in 1933.

In the 1940s, black pilots trained at the Tuskegee Army Air Field in Alabama and became distinguished fighters in World War II, dispelling the myth that black aviators were not capable of combat flying. The success of the Tuskegee Airmen provided an incentive for the United States government to desegregate its armed forces.

I hope that you will go to the library and read more about these and other black aviators. But before you do, a quick lesson in flying: Close your eyes. Imagine that you're floating through the air, climbing toward the sky. Once you're as high as you want to go, go a little bit higher. Look around. What do you see? Think about a place you've always dreamed of going, something you've always wanted to do. Go there, do that. And remember your adventures, so that you will be able to experience them all over again, this time with your eyes open. Live your dreams. Never let anyone clip your wings. Happy flying!

—N.A.T.